Puffin Books
Brinsly's Dream

'Anybody in the world can play football,' said Brinsly's sister, but Brinsly knew there was more to it than that, much, *much* more.

Brinsly just lived for football, and he knew his team had got to practise really hard, not just kick a ball about in fun, if they were going to win a few matches, maybe even win the festival trophy!

It was going to be hard work to get the sisters organized into knitting team scarves, the mothers providing food, and above all to make the lads turn out without fail for every practice, but Brinsly was prepared to give it every ounce of energy he had. But what he hadn't bargained for was that he might actually run into danger from the other side's jealous supporters!

A good exciting story about a boy, his friends, and, of course, football. Just right for eight- and nine-year-olds.

Petronella Breinburg

BRINSLY'S DREAM

Illustrated by Robert Hales

Puffin Books

For Carl and all the boys and girls of
Plumcraft Junior School, Plumstead, London s.e.18

Puffin Books, Penguin Books Ltd, Harmondsworth, Middlesex, England
Penguin Books, 625 Madison Avenue, New York,
New York 10022, U.S.A.
Penguin Books Australia Ltd, Ringwood, Victoria, Australia
Penguin Books Canada Ltd, 2801 John Street, Markham,
Ontario, Canada l3r 1b4
Penguin Books (N.Z.) Ltd, 182–190 Wairau Road,
Auckland 10, New Zealand

First published by Burke Books 1976
Published in Puffin Books 1980

Made and printed in Great Britain by
Richard Clay (The Chaucer Press) Ltd, Bungay, Suffolk
Set in Monotype Garamond

Contents

1 Sugar-Cake 7
2 The Errand 10
3 Seven-a-Side 12
4 The Popapoulos Boys 16
5 Five Nil 19
6 Brinsly in Trouble 23
7 Plans 26
8 A Visit from Nevil 29
9 Late! 33
10 The Practice 39
11 The Best Goalie in the World 47
12 The Visit to Aunt Doreen 54
13 New Colours 70
14 The Game with Charlton 75
15 The Trophy 84

1 Sugar-Cake

Mother was making 'sugar-cake'. Brinsly knew that the moment he walked in.

'Mh, mh, nice!' Brinsly sniffed.

There was that sweet smell of essence, vanilla essence it was, too. And of sugar and coconut being boiled.

'Smells good!' Brinsly grinned.

Suddenly Brinsly remembered that he had not wiped his feet. His mother was very fussy about people wiping their feet each time they came in from outside.

'Mah! Mum!' Brinsly quickly stamped on the mat. He felt that stamping on the mat was as good as wiping your feet. So he stamped, leaning forward a little. He stamped first with his right foot, then his left, and his 'feet wiping' ceremony was over.

Brinsly hurried to the kitchen because he could hear Patricia's voice. Patricia was, no doubt, helping Mother.

'I'm home, Mum,' Brinsly called and ran up to his mother.

'Hi! Watch it!' his mother cried. 'You'll get burnt, boy.' His mother came quickly between him and the saucepan steaming from the cooker. And the smell of essence! Brinsly could hardly wait to get his teeth on the sugar-cake.

Not too far away Patricia was getting the wooden tray ready. On this tray Mother would mould the boiled coconut and sugar into small cakes.

'Got m' book?' Patricia asked Brinsly.

'Yeh, got one on witches. You like witches. That's what I got you anyway. You don't expect me to find girls' books. I'd look stupid looking for a girl's book.'

'What's stupid about that? I get your books when you go to Cubs, don't I?'

'Look out!'

Mother was ready to take the saucepan off the cooker. 'You better . . . oh!'

Mother suddenly remembered, 'Didn't have time today to chip up the coconut, so it's grated today. Been at the launderette for hours. Everybody seem to want to do their washing on same day.'

2 The Errand

Brinsly was not to taste that day's delicacy yet though. He found that he had an errand to do first.

'Nearly forgot,' Mother said. 'You dad want you to get this.'

Mother then fished out a slip of paper from her apron pocket.

'Here's the money for it.'

Mother's fingers dived into her purse which always seemed to stand on the kitchen shelf.

'Why can't Patricia go?' Brinsly protested bitterly. He felt that he always had to do everything. 'Why can't *she* go?'

'I've got to help in the house ... see?' said Patricia spitefully, pulling a face at her younger brother.

'Anybody can help in the house. There's nothing to do in the house ...'

'Enough! Don't want to listen to you two at it again. The way you go on and on, you'll drive me to the mad house!' said Mother.

'He started it,' said Patricia.

'It's you who started it,' said Brinsly.

'Out with you,' said Mother and ushered Brinsly to the door. 'Now you run along like a good little boy and get that thing for your father, eh? He said to go to that electric shop by The Dip.'

'All right, all right. I'll go, I'll go.' Brinsly was very upset at having to leave the sugar-cake. 'Let all the cakes get stone cold. Don't care! Let them get stone cold.'

'They *will* get stone cold if you stand there moping. Hurry 'long. Watch the traffic. You hear me?' Mother shouted after Brinsly. 'Watch how you cross!'

3   Seven-a-Side

Brinsly first walked as slowly as he could. 'Don't care if the sugar-cakes get cold,' he sulked.

Then suddenly he told himself, 'What's the use of walking slow? I'll run. I'll dash through Plum Lane, down to the park, cross quickly. Not much traffic at this time. Then I can get back home quick ...' Brinsly began to run.

So deep in thought was Brinsly that he didn't notice his best pals kicking a ball down Plum Lane.

'Brinsly! Brin ... !' The pals shouted all together.

Brinsly heard them and stood still. He was panting a little though. It was downhill but a very steep hill. You had to be careful and keep yourself from falling flat on your face.

'Hi,' said Clive.

'Hi,' said Brinsly.

'Where're you going?' asked Mark.

'Got a match,' said Paul.

'And we need a good goalie,' said Clive.

'Yeh. A good one like you. Coming?' asked Mark.

'Can't – got to get this fuse. M' Dad going to need it.' Brinsly finally got a word in.

'You can get it later,' said Clive. 'Come on! We're playing those Popapoulos brothers.'

'Not them?' cried Brinsly, horrified.

'Yes, them. All six of them're coming. Say we, say we – they're saying terrible things,' Clive said.

'Say . . . tell him?' asked Mark.

'Yes, tell Brinsly what they're saying about Shrewsbury Hill boys,' said Clive.

'Said we can't play ball, we can only play old ladies.'

'No! They said that?' Brinsly could not believe it.

'Yeh. Say they can prove it too. So if we don't turn up . . .' said Clive.

'Yes. That would show that we're scared, they'll call us chicken,' said Paul.

'Oh go on, Brins . . . we need more men . . . only, let me see, one, two. Only four of us,' said Mark.

'We can go and fetch that new boy. You know . . . that one who speaks Jamaican, what's his name? You know him . . . goes to Bloomfield's,' said Paul.

'Ah, him. He's big. Bigger than us,' said Brinsly.

'He's only first year though. My brother is first year and my brother's only eleven,' said Clive.

By this time the boys had reached the end of Plum Lane.

'Eh, what about them Garrot boys? Two of 'em. They live down there,' Brinsly pointed to a side street.

'What if you went and got that boy who speaks Jamaican and I'll go and get the Garrot boys?' said Paul.

'That would be how many men?' asked Mark.

'That would be seven, not enough for a full team but too much for five-a-side,' explained Brinsly.

'We have seven-a-side then. Serve the Popapoulos

boys right. Let them have one less. And with you in goal . . . they'll see who are old ladies,' said Paul.

So, while Paul and Mark went to fetch the Garrot brothers, Brinsly and Clive went to fetch the boy who spoke Jamaican.

When the two other boys were out of earshot, Brinsly asked, 'Think we'll win?'

'Don't think so,' said Clive, 'but Paul insists, says they'll call us chickens if we don't show up at all. But everybody knows no one can beat those Popapoulos brothers. Not even the littlest one. They say he's only six. And you see what he can do with a ball, man?'

4   The Popapoulos Boys

The Shrewsbury Hill boys finally gathered up a team.
There were eleven men and two footballs. They arrived
at the zebra crossing to find that the Popapoulos brothers
were already on the common.

'Now listen,' Brinsly warned his men, 'they say
things in Greek. Don't worry if you can't understand.
When they say something in Greek you know that's
when you got to watch them.'

'You mean dem planning a trick?' asked the boy
who spoke Jamaican.

'Yeh. They make signs as well,' explained Mark.

'And they do dummies. Remember that. Cross
now,' said Brinsly, indicating that the road was now
clear.

'What is dummy?' asked the boy who spoke Jamaican.

The Popapoulos boys were too busy doing things with
the ball to notice the arrival of the Shrewsbury Hill boys.

The Greek brothers were heading the ball from one
brother's head to the other. They were doing it so fast
you could hardly see what colour the ball was. And if
you looked too long at the ball it made you dizzy. As for
the littlest brother, he even spun around while the ball
was going round and turned back just in time to catch it
with the back of his head. He had to bend his head to it

but he got it. He then headed the ball back to the next brother.

'Christ!' cried the boy who spoke Jamaican.

'Hi, that's swearing,' warned Brinsly, but Brinsly had no time left to explain to his pal, for the Greek brothers had spotted them.

'So you turn up?' one of the Popapoulos brothers grinned.

'Yeh. They turn up,' mocked the youngest brother. 'Or have you fellows changed your minds? Mind you, I wouldn't blame you if you had . . .'

'Leh we start now,' said the boy who spoke Jamaican.

'What's that he said?' asked one of the Popapoulos brothers.

'Said we're ready for you Barnsfield Boosters,' said Brinsly angrily.

'Good. Which goal-posts d'you want?' said one of the Popapoulos brothers. 'Left or right?'

'That one.' Brinsly pointed to one side of the common.

'Which side breeze'eh blowing?' whispered the boy who spoke Jamaican.

'Don't know,' said Clive.

'What has the breeze got to do with football?' asked Mark.

'Anyhow we start,' said Brinsly. 'Now don't be afraid of them,' Brinsly reminded himself. 'Worst thing you can do is to be afraid. Dad always said so. Never be afraid. You're as good as the next man.'

But Brinsly was afraid. Just a little bit. This was because the Popapoulos brothers were the best in Plumstead. The best in the whole world even.

'Come on! Are you afraid?' called the fattest of the Greek brothers.

'Of course we're not!' called Clive.

'You watch and see whether we're afraid!' said Brinsly.

5   Five Nil

That afternoon Brinsly played as he had never played before. Very soon the Shrewsbury boys were three goals down yet Brinsly fought on. By that time, one of Brinsly's own men had decided to join on the winning boys' side. Yet Brinsly tried. He saved many goals. Once a hard ball nearly blew his head off. It had struck him hard on the temple. Yet Brinsley saved the goal. He just managed to push it away from the coats serving as goalposts.

But Brinsly could not play the game alone. True, he had the boy who spoke Jamaican fighting hard too. The boy was older so his legs were longer and occasionally he managed to grab the ball away from these feared brothers.

Most of the other men in Brinsly's team were afraid to tackle. Sometimes Clive would be very near scoring and Brinsly would shout, 'Go on, Clive. Idiot, score! Score!' But Clive never got past the fattish Popapoulos in goal. Denos, that was his name. Denos often threw his big body across and stopped the ball with his broad chest. Denos was the best goalkeeper in the world. But also, Clive was afraid to tackle Denos.

At one time Brinsly thought of taking Clive's place and putting someone else in goal but the other men disagreed. 'If you leave the goal they'll score one hundred,' they all said.

In the end, it was the Popapoulos brothers who said they had to go home now. By that time, the score was five nil in favour of the Greek boys. It could have been fifty nil if Brinsly had not saved so many.

So, heavy-hearted, Brinsly and the Shrewsbury Hill boys went home. They said very little. Once or twice the boy who spoke Jamaican told them that they needed to practise more. They must practise every day and only amongst themselves. If they did this they too could make signs to each other. The boy explained that twice he was trying to tell Clive to pass the ball to him but Clive could not understand. 'Also,' said the boy who spoke Jamaican, 'you scare of them man, done be scare and practise, you scare, man!'

'We'll practise every day,' all the men agreed. 'To-morrow is Saturday, we meet at eleven, right? Right!'

Not at the Plumstead Common, they all agreed. They'd meet in Shrewsbury Park. By that big gate.

The boys then parted and Brinsly went home to find his mother terribly angry about something.

'So you finally come home!' Mother screamed at him. She placed her hands on her hips and stared murderously at him.

'So you finally come home! Don't have to ask where you been. Can tell from you filthy clothes. Here is your father waiting for this fuse to do m' iron.'

'Dad? Dad!' Brinsly wanted to scream the words but they came out only as a whisper.

'Yes, Dad! Went looking for you!' said Patricia. 'Found the shops all closed.'

'And me with all this ironing to do,' said Mother, her hands still on her hips. 'Now let me have that fuse. Maybe Mr Forbes next door can do the iron for me. Don't know when your dad'll be back.'

'Went out really mad,' added Patricia. 'He's really mad. Better warn you! Said he'll kill you, dead!'

'Come, hand me that fuse, boy!' Mother was still very angry.

But Brinsly had nothing to hand over. He'd never got to the shop. He wanted to explain to his mother what had happened. He wanted to explain that he had forgotten all about the fuse he went to buy, but no words came.

He tried hard to speak but each time a word tried to get out a big lump pushed it back down. His throat felt terribly dry as well. He had been shrieking and shouting for nearly an hour. He had had nothing to drink since the 'home' bell went at school and that was a long time ago. And the way his mother was looking at him, and the way Patricia said that Dad was really mad, all these made him feel faint. His mother had plenty of clothes to iron and needed her iron, but an iron cannot work without its fuse, so it seemed anyway. It was then that Brinsly's hand went to his pocket . . . The money . . .? He was not sure if he actually said the words aloud.

'Could run away to Aunt Myrtle! No, I'd have to get a train. No money. They don't let you out the train station without a ticket. My piggy bank's almost empty. Sometimes the bus conductors in Hackney used to give kids a little ride on their bus, but the ones in Plumstead don't. If you try to get a ride they shout, "Get off!" They say, "No money, no bus ride." Besides, if I run away I wouldn't be at the park tomorrow and they will be short of a goalie. We got to beat those Popapoulos brothers. Got to. If we practise hard, whole day perhaps. I can start practising early tomorrow morning. I always wake up very early before everyone else. So instead of lying in bed I'll get up and go out to Shrewsbury Park and practise.'

8   A Visit from Nevil

In the end Brinsly decided that he could not run away.
If he did run away he would be letting the others down.
So he waited. He was sure that Dad would come and
fetch him. Dad would not let him spend the night
in an old shed. But what if Dad thought he had run
away?

'Brinsly . . . come out from there, Brinsly!' It was
Dad's voice and what's more he did not sound mad any
more.

So Brinsly crawled out from the shed – and about time
too, because his legs were beginning to hurt. He was not
exactly comfortable in that shed full of junk. And the
shed smelt a bit too.

'What you want to run for?' asked Dad as he helped
Brinsly up. 'Some friends here to see you anyway. Your
football friends.'

When Dad and Brinsly got inside the house they
found that Mother was already placing sugar-cakes in
front of the guests. Brinsly recognized the boy from
Jamaica but he did not know the older boy.

'Now.' Mother grinned in her usual way. 'What do
you know? This nice young man want to teach you kids
to play football.' Mother looked proudly at the very
tall boy. 'To play properly.'

Brinsly gasped and wondered if he was still in the shed and had fallen asleep. 'I always dream things,' said Brinsly to himself. 'That time I dreamt it all that I went to the school outing. I didn't though. Ma could not afford the money that time.'

'Hi,' said Brinsly because he didn't know what else to say.

'Hi. I am Nevil and I am Lloyd's uncle. I am trying to get a football team going. I work at the club . . . you know the club near the church? In Burrage Road.'

'He knows. He knows the place, don't you?' said Mother quickly.

'I know,' said Patricia. 'Some of the girls from my class go there for dancing.'

'See,' said Mother. 'I tell you he knows. Have another cake. Have another as well.' Mother proudly passed the dish around.

'Go on,' said Dad. 'You know the place.'

'Yes. I know but . . . got to go to Cubs and . . .'

'What days do you go to Cubs?' asked Nevil.

'Mondays.'

'Good. Because we'll be training every *Saturday* at Shrewsbury Park. Eleven o'clock sharp. Think you can make it? You'll have to get up early. You will have to work hard, too, very hard.'

Brinsly could not believe it. When the visitors had left Brinsly asked Patricia to pinch him so that he could see if he was not dreaming it all. Patricia pinched him hard. Brinsly yelled sharply. He knew then that it was not one of his dreams. He was really going to learn how to play the game. And would he play! Popapoulos brothers or no Popapoulos brothers.

That night Brinsly went to bed happy. The spot where the ball hit him still hurt a bit. But he was happy. Smiling, he took out the sugar-cake he had hidden in his pocket. He munched it. He'd play football well. His team would always play well. He told himself that he must sleep now. He'd be able to get out of bed early, then. Very early. He'd have to shine his football boots, they were somewhere in the cupboard. And what of his football kit? His things should be clean. Mother always washed them as soon as he returned from school games.

What time should he get up? he wondered. Maybe seven! Would Mother call him as usual? What if she forgot to call him and he got to the park too late? They'd all be gone then. They'd say, 'Brinsly isn't coming, let's all go home.'

No, Mother would call him, or send Patricia to call him.

9   Late!

'Brinsly, Brin!' called Patricia. 'It's late. You've over-slept, Brinsly.'

Quickly Brinsly got out of bed. He rubbed his eyes. He always rubbed his eyes to help him wake up. Then he noticed that there was something wrong. He was not too sure at first what it was that was wrong. But he later saw what it was. He had not undressed before he went to bed the night before. He had slept in his clothes. And he had his shoes on too. All he needed to do now was to race downstairs and get his football boots out of the cupboard.

He called out to his dad, 'Dad, Dad, can you take me to the park, please? I'm late.' When his dad did not answer, Brinsly thought that he had already gone out. So he raced downstairs. Then he noticed. The whole passage was empty. The cupboard which once held his football boots was also empty. The vacuum cleaner was gone, the brooms, the dustpans, everything was gone.

'Mum!' called Brinsly. He rushed to the kitchen where he hoped to find Mother. But Mother was not there. There was nothing there. The cooker, the spin dryer, everything was gone. The chairs, tables, even Mother's purse which always stood on the mantelpiece was gone.

'Patricia, Pat!' called Brinsly and ran out to the garden. But Patricia was nowhere to be seen.

Suddenly, Brinsly heard the noise of a car outside. He thought that it sounded like his dad's car. His dad was about to drive away. Brinsly rushed to the front door.

'Dad, Dad,' he cried. 'Wait for me, Dad!'

'Well, hurry up. We haven't got all day,' said Dad.

Brinsly ran down the stone steps, jumped into the back seat of the car, slammed the door closed just in time before Dad drove off. Only when they drove off did Brinsly notice that there was a removal van in front of them. Dad was trying to keep close behind the van. Brinsly was about to ask Dad why they were moving when the back door of the van flew open.

There were people in the van. They began to cheer and shout. There were hundreds of people. All dressed in red-and-white scarves and berets. There were all the boys from Brinsly's school, from Plum Lane Juniors. The infants weren't there. There was also that boy who spoke Jamaican, his uncle, and the Popapoulos brothers.

The brothers were shouting, 'Shrewsbury boys rule, O.K.?'

Then Brinsly's dad shouted back to the brothers, 'Shrewsbury boys rule, O.K.?'

'O.K.,' shouted all the people in the van.

Only then did Brinsly notice that his dad was also dressed in a red-and-white scarf and hat. But when Brinsly looked down to his own clothes he was horrified. He was still in his pyjamas. He couldn't understand it. He was sure that he went to sleep in his day clothes.

'Dad, Dad,' cried Brinsly, 'I'm still in my pyjamas, Dad. I can't go in my pyjamas.'

But Dad was not listening. He drove as fast as he could, and got to the football pitch just after the removal van full of Shrewsbury fans.

Brinsly had no time to argue further about his pyjamas for the fans jumped out of the van and came to lift Brinsly out of the car.

'Hurry up,' said a man at the gate. 'You're late. The whole team is already here.'

'But, but . . .' Brinsly began but he was pushed on to the field. A band was already playing. Then Brinsly saw them. His sister Patricia and her school friends, and lots of girls from Plum Lane Junior School. They were pretending to be majorettes. They were dressed in majorette costume and were waving batons. Patricia was in the lead and waving a huge baton. The crowd cheered. The band followed the majorettes.

Then, to Brinsly's horror, he saw his mother. His mother was banging a huge drum. The drum was sitting on Mother's chest and looked much too heavy for her. But Mother smiled and banged away.

Brinsly made as if to run up to Mother but the whistle blew for the kick-off. The game began.

Brinsly was in goal as usual. But he never had to work so hard. Balls seemed to come at him from all directions. He jumped, headed, dived from side to side, the crowd roared. They chanted:

'Come on, goalie,' *clap*, *clap*.

'Come on, goalie,' *clap*, *clap*.

'Come on, goalie,' *clap*, *clap*.

Brinsly felt tired, yet he kept on. Balls from the right were saved, balls from the left were saved too and the high balls were headed. In the end, Brinsly felt so tired he just could not go on any more. He badly wanted to sit down or simply lie down and go to sleep. He felt his eyes closing. The cheers from the fans got further and further away. He felt himself slipping to the ground. He told himself that he must keep on. He could not though. He just fell down.

He didn't know how long he had lain there. The next thing he knew was Mother shaking him.

'Wake up, Brinsly! Brinsly, what's the matter?' Mother's voice sounded far away.

'Brinsly, you've been sleeping on the floor. And in your house clothes too,' said Patricia.

'What's the matter?' asked Dad from the doorway.

'He fell asleep on the bare floor. Could've been there all night,' said Mother.

'And he been eating in his bedroom,' said Patricia. 'Look, sugar-cake and biscuit!'

'Oh, leave him alone,' said Dad.

'Oh, what time is it? When did I get back?' Brinsly rubbed his eyes.

'Back from where?' asked Patricia.

'Wakey, wakey, it's after eight. We let you sleep, but when you didn't come down I came to call you,' said Mother.

'And there you were sleeping in your house clothes and eating in your bedroom,' repeated Patricia spitefully.

'He was in his pyjamas when I came to tuck him in last night,' said Mother.

'Strange,' said Dad. 'But you better hurry, if you people want me to take you shopping.'

'What day is it, then?' asked Brinsly.

'Saturday, silly,' said Patricia.

'Oh, Saturday! I got to be at Shrewsbury Park at eleven. Do I have to go shopping, Mum?'

'No, you got to come and help. I can't do all the chores,' said Patricia.

The Practice

Brinsly did not go to help with the shopping that day. Dad said that he could stay in and get ready for his first football practice. So while Dad took the family to Woolwich Market, Brinsly was left alone. He polished his football boots and got his kit ready. It was only just gone ten when he arrived at Shrewsbury Park.

'I'll practise a bit until they arrive,' he told himself. He tried a few high kicks, but found that to practise saving he needed someone to kick the ball at him. He then thought that he had better run down the hill and get Clive. Clive should be ready by now, anyway.

But when Brinsly knocked at Clive's door, there was no answer.

'He must have gone up the other way,' thought Brinsly, so he ran as fast as he could to the park. But there was no Clive. In fact, there was only the old lady and a dog whom Brinsly had seen earlier on.

'Eh, mister,' called Brinsly to a man, 'have you seen a boy, eh, same age like me?'

'I've seen hundreds of boys same age, like you.'

Suddenly, Brinsly thought that he had better pinch himself. Maybe he was dreaming again. He felt the pinch so he was not dreaming.

He saw a lady with a dog. He asked: 'Eh, please, lady, what time is it?'

'Oh, the time? Let me see now. Twenty-five past ten,' said the lady.

'That's all?'

'I'm afraid so, why?'

'Got to meet my team mates at eleven,' said Brinsly and went to stroke the dog.

'Oh, a long wait I'm afraid,' said the old lady.

'I better go and see where they are.'

'What if you went and they came another way? They'll think that you're not coming.'

'Oh,' said Brinsly, 'I better stay and wait then.'

'I should think so. Are you having a match of some kind? My grandson is always having matches, he's a goalie, so I believe.'

'Oh no, not a proper match, not yet. We got to practise first. We got to learn to play the game right.'

'That's right, you must learn and never give up trying. You'll lose sometimes. Sometimes you'll lose, but never give up.'

'But what if you lose all the time?'

'Still keep on trying, you're bound to win one day. Oh, dear, I'd better get home. Susie! Susie, Susie!' the old lady called to her dog.

Left alone once more, Brinsly wondered if he should wait any longer. Maybe he had made a mistake about the place they were to meet. Maybe it was at the Centre by the church, not Shrewsbury Park that they were to meet. He looked round for someone else to ask the time from, but there was no one else now. All the old ladies and dogs had gone.

'Maybe I'm at the wrong gate,' he thought. 'That's it! There are so many entrances.'

So Brinsly ran to the other entrance, the one by the library, but there was no one there. He ran back to the main entrance and then he saw them.

'Here, here, I'm here!' called Brinsly.

'Hi,' called the boy who spoke Jamaican. 'We early.'

Brinsly took it that the boy was asking if they were early.

'No, it's gone eleven,' said Brinsly, sadly looking to the gate to see if the others were coming.

'Quarter to, exactly,' said Nevil. 'But my nephew here wouldn't let me sleep. Nearly brought me out in the middle of the night.' Nevil pretended to yawn.

'Me didn't know it was midnight. London always

dark,' said the boy in Jamaican language, but Brinsly understood him, a little.

'Hi, look, them Popapoulos boys. But what are they doing here?' cried Brinsly.

'I've been to see their parents as well,' explained Nevil.

'But you're not going to teach them?' asked Brinsly.

'I am. Then we can form a proper team.'

'But they can play already and they don't live near Shrewsbury Park,' said Brinsly.

Secretly he was angry. He was hoping to practise so as to beat those boastful Popapoulos boys.

'Hi,' said Nevil to the brothers.

There were only the four youngest of the brothers, Brinsly was quick to notice. But even the younger ones could already play well, so why teach them? And they boasted too much. Always saying that Brinsly's team could only win against old ladies.

But that day the brothers weren't talking much. They explained that the older two brothers had to stay and help in their dad's shop. Besides, they were in secondary school already. They didn't want to play junior boys.

'Oh, he is an infant,' protested Brinsly, pointing to the youngest boy. He was still sulking about the boys coming at all. 'See, he's an infant.'

'I can play though, even if I'm only in the Infants, I can kick, mister,' said the youngest of the brothers. 'I *can*, you try me out.'

'Nevil. The name is Nevil. But where *are* the others?'

'Don't know,' said Brinsly. 'I've been to Clive's house but he wasn't there. No one answered the door.'

'Maybe they were still asleep,' said one of the brothers.

'His mum sometimes works nights. She works at the hospital up the hill, see.'

'Shall I go and see again?' asked Brinsly.

'Well, I suppose so,' said Nevil, looking again at the big clock in the park. 'But I did tell them eleven o'clock and now it is gone that.'

'Well, I'll go and see,' said Brinsly.

'Coming with you,' said one of the brothers.

'No,' said Brinsly sharply. He was still angry about the brothers being there.

'Me coming with you,' said the boy in Jamaican.

'All right then.' And Brinsly wondered if he should correct the boy. Maybe he should tell the boy that in England people didn't say 'Me coming'.

'Me name Errol,' said the boy when Brinsly didn't say anything else.

'My name is Brinsly,' said Brinsly with a smile. 'But let's hurry and fetch them.'

They got to Clive's house, but when they rang the upstairs bell for Clive, again there was no answer. They rang and rang. Then a head poked through the window downstairs. It was one of Clive's neighbours.

An angry voice called, 'Stop making that noise. Clive's gone to his granny. Don't come ringing again. There're people in this house on night duty!' Then the window slammed closed.

'What wrong with she?' asked Errol.

'We say, "What's wrong with her!"' laughed Brinsly. 'Anyway, let's go to the Garrots.'

But when Brinsly and Errol got there they were told that the boys could not come. Saturday was a busy day. The boys had to help run errands.

Brinsly and Errol ran all the way to Paul's house. But Paul too could not come. He had to help his dad repair the shed.

So the only man left to fetch was Mark.

'He's gone,' said Mark's mother. 'Just left. Got up late as usual, then he found his football kit filthy, then . . .'

Brinsly and Errol did not hear what Mark's mother had to say. They ran to Shrewsbury Park. There they found the brothers and Mark having a meeting with Nevil.

'Sit down, men,' said Nevil.

Brinsly sat down, but he told himself that he wished Nevil would hurry and start the practice session.

Nevil was explaining lots of things about how to kick a ball. Brinsly thought that was a bit silly. Everybody in the world knew how to kick a ball. You just put your foot against it and kick. But Nevil had other ideas. He said that you had to kick the ball from under it.

A long time passed. By then Brinsly was fed up with talks. He wanted to get on with the game. In the end, Nevil said that they should have a practice on what they were just discussing. Brinsly felt terrible. He was not concentrating. He was so busy thinking about winning the game he was not listening properly so he didn't know what to do.

He tried to kick the way he always did, but Nevil didn't seem to like that. 'Look, like this. Watch me.'

Brinsly was horrified. Nevil was actually demonstrating with one of the Popapoulos brothers. The boy had been listening and was doing exactly what Nevil had been telling him to do.

44

'See, now you have a go! Brinsly and Denos, it is Denos, isn't it?'

'Yes, it is. And he is Carlo . . .'

'Oh dear, it will take me years to tell one brother from the other,' laughed Nevil. 'But carry on. You and Brinsly practise passing. Errol and Mark here will shadow you. They'll try to stop you getting the ball to each other. Get it?'

But no matter how hard Brinsly tried, he got it all wrong. He first blamed it on the fact that Errol was older and he had longer legs. So he stopped the ball long before it got to Brinsly. And then Denos was blaming it all on Brinsly and kept shouting at him. Besides, Brinsly thought, if he was only going to be a goalie why should he do all that 'passing' stuff. He just wanted to learn to stop the ball getting in the net, that's all. In the end, Brinsly decided that the whole practice session was boring. He then played so badly that Nevil thought that it was time to go home. They'd meet again next Saturday, when perhaps Brinsly would be concentrating better.

Sadly, and feeling all fed up, Brinsly got home. There he was told by his sister that the whole idea was stupid. Anybody in the world can play football!

11 The Best Goalie in the World

The next day was Sunday. Brinsly did not have to get up early but he did. He could not wait to get to the others. He was going to tell them off good and proper.

The first doorbell Brinsly rang was Paul's.

Paul was still in his pyjamas when he came to the door and he was rubbing his eyes.

'Mh,' Paul yawned. 'Why you ring so early? M' dad don't like people ringing so early.'

'It's not early. It's gone nine. And you didn't show up at all. I was looking for you all day yesterday.'

Just then, a voice called from inside the house. It was Paul's mother. 'Paul, come in here this moment. And close that door, will you? It's draughty in here.'

'Got to go now,' said Paul. 'Come back later. About four o'clock. I'll finish m' dinner by then.'

Paul went inside and Brinsly turned sadly away. How he wished he had some men he could depend on. Nevil had warned that unless they worked hard as a team they'd never win any matches. But how could they work as a team if the men didn't turn up?

Brinsly decided to go home, get his ball and practise on his own. But when he got to Shrewsbury Park, the Popapoulos brothers were all there kicking. What's more, they had some older men with them. This made

47

Brinsly very angry. No wonder the brothers played so well. They were having the help of older men.

Angrily, Brinsly stood by a tree and watched the game going on. He blamed his dad. Why couldn't his dad be like these dads here kicking the ball and teaching their children the game?

Suddenly, one of the older men nearly scored a goal. The fastest of the Popapoulos dived, saved it. Someone cheered, 'Well saved!'

Brinsly looked round and saw that it was the old lady again. She saw Brinsly watching and waved to him. Brinsly waved back. The old lady called out something which Brinsly couldn't understand so Brinsly went up to her.

'What did you say?' asked Brinsly.

'Why aren't you there kicking, lad? Go on, get in there and show 'em.'

Well, Brinsly thought carefully. He did not want to be in the same team with the Popapoulos but there was no harm just playing with them.

Brinsly walked up and asked, 'Can I have a game?'

'Hi, Brin, that's Brinsly,' cried Denos 'He's the best goalie in Plumstead.'

'The whole world,' said the brother in goal. 'Take over in goal, Brin!'

'Well,' Brinsly was not too sure.

'Go on,' cried one of the men. 'You gone chicken, or something?'

'Hurry, Brinsly, it's dads against sons,' said Denos.

'Dads and uncles,' said one of the men.

At once Brinsly got in the goal. It was hard work trying to stop the balls getting in. The men were

tackling very hard and they had huge legs. Many times Brinsly had to throw his whole body on the ball to stop those long legs getting it in.

Many times he told himself that it was unfair. Those were big men. How could young boys beat them? Once Brinsly got a hard kick on his ankle and felt like crying but he held the tears back. Another time he fell on his hand and hurt his wrist, yet he stayed on. In the end the men thought that it was time to go home. The score then was dads and uncles: four. Sons and friends: two.

'You worked hard,' said one of the dads. 'But be careful with laying on the ball like that. You can get your face kicked in.'

'He won't, he's the best goalie in the world,' said Denos.

Brinsly waved good-bye to the men and the brothers and then limped his way home. As soon as he got home he knew that he was in trouble. He knew because Mum did not answer when he spoke to her and her face looked as if she was cross. It was Patricia who whispered, 'You in trouble, again.'

'What for? What did I do?'

'What you did? You walked out the house and told nobody anything, that's what.'

'But you were all asleep.'

'I wasn't. I heard you close the front door, see.'

'Well . . . anyway, I went to play football.'

'Football, football, that's all you can think of.'

'What about you and your stupid dolls and things, them things that can't talk or do anything.'

'Balls can't talk neither.'

'Don't care. I like football. Going to play for, eh, Millwall, or Chelsea. See!'

'Dad's going to Chelsea you, don't worry. You running off like that and worrying Mum.'

'Worry, why should she worry?'

'You wasn't in your bed, that's why. You could have been kidnapped.'

'Kidnapped, what for?'

'Don't know, for money, that's it. Someone wants Dad to steal the post office money, so they kidnap you. Oh, that's Dad now. I'm going upstairs; got to do my chores.'

'Dad, hi, Dad, been to practise my goalkeeping,' Brinsly said, hoping that his dad would be pleased.

'Saved many goal and they were big men too, dads and uncles they were.'

At first, Brinsly thought that Dad was not going to speak to him. Dad had gone to the kitchen to fill a pail with water. He was washing his car at the back. Brinsly followed Dad to the back.

'I'll help you, can I?'

'You may if you want, but that wouldn't help.'

'I only went to practise, Dad. We can't make a good team if we don't practise.'

'True, but you can't just drop everything and go.'

'Sorry, Dad.'

'What about your breakfast?'

'Oh, breakfast, that's why I feel so hungry; had no breakfast.'

Brinsly hurried back in the house. There he apologized to his mother.

'Sorry I worried you, Mum. But –' Brinsly laughed '– no one going to kidnap me, Mum, not unless I become a great footballer, and I may too!'

'Great footballer, indeed,' mocked Patricia. 'You better help do some work. I got to do it all. I'll never finish in time for Brownie sing-song . . . and . . .'

'All right, don't want to hear any more moans. Kidnap indeed. You Brinsly, hurry up and have your breakfast,' said his mother. Brinsly knew that Mum was no longer cross.

'All right, Mum. I'll clean the windows for you, as soon as I've finished.'

'Yeh, and clean the mess you and your friends made by the back gates,' said Patricia.

'What about the mess your friends make?'

'Your friends are more messy.'

'That's enough,' said Mother. 'Get going, Brinsly, and you too, Patricia.'

'She's always saying things about my friends,' Brinsly wanted to have the last word.

'Shut up,' shouted Mother.

Brinsly pulled a face at his sister before he ran up to the kitchen where the smell of fried bacon filled his nose. He felt terribly hungry then and told himself that next time he'd make sure he had a good breakfast before he went out to practise.

'Can't practise on an empty stomach or you'll faint and lose the game,' he thought.

12 The Visit to Aunt Doreen

After Brinsly had eaten, he thought that he'd help round the house like a good boy. Then he would be able to run out again and find his men. He must find out why they did not turn up. He would warn them that, no matter what happened, they must turn up for practice.

Brinsly helped Mother clean all the windows at the front of the house. All the time he was helping he thought about going out again.

Soon it was time for lunch. Mother got a lovely juicy chicken out of the oven. Again Brinsly helped, and without being told. He helped to lay the table. This gave Patricia a big shock.

'Eh? Brinsly helping with the table?' Patricia sneered.

'I am. So what? My teacher says the best chefs are men, so there!' He laughed because for once he did not want to argue with his sister.

Lunch was lovely and Brinsly helped clear up afterwards. Mother said that they could leave the dishes in the sink. She'd do them when they came back.

'Come back?' asked Brinsly, horrified.

'Yes, when we come back from Aunty Doreen,' she said.

'Cor, can't wait to see the new cousin,' said Patricia.

'Can't we go later, this evening?' asked Dad.

At once Brinsly joined in with his father. 'Yes, let's go tonight.'

'Babies sleep at night,' said Patricia. 'Besides, we wouldn't be able to see her properly.'

'Well, all right then, but I can stay behind. I can see the baby another time.'

'Oh no, you can't! We're all going,' said Patricia.

'But I don't want to go. I hate babies, anyway.'

'Brinsly, since when is it that you start to hate babies, eh?' asked Mother, puzzled.

'All the time. They're always screaming, and they smell.'

'Brinsly!' shouted Mother.

'He's only saying that because he wants to go outside with his mates,' said Patricia.

'I must say this for him though,' Dad cleared his throat. 'He worked very hard today, didn't you, son?'

'Good! He'll get a big ice-cream when we get on the road. Now hurry up, you two men! We ladies will be ready soon.'

Mother went upstairs to change into her best dress. Patricia followed. She too had to get into her best frock. Dad looked at Brinsly and shook his head. 'I tried to help, son,' he said. Then he got up. 'But, well, we better get ready.'

'But I don't want to go, Dad. I can stay here alone. I'll be good, honest.'

'Son, when Mum says we go to see the new baby, we have to go to see the new baby.' Dad patted Brinsly on the shoulder.

'I hate babies. I wish all babies would drop dead!'

'Now now, I'm sure you don't mean that. Now hurry,

maybe you'll get a game by your aunt's place. I always see boys kicking a ball in the park by Blackheath.'

But Brinsly did not want to kick a ball with boys in Blackheath. He wanted to find his own men and give them a talking-to. Maybe he could even have had a quick practice.

All the way to Aunt Doreen, Brinsly sulked. 'Why do I have to have relations?' he sulked. 'Aunties and screaming babies.'

It would not have been so bad if he had some cousins who were old enough to play football. But to have screaming babies as cousins, that was terrible. And some of the babies smell. That's because they are sick on their bibs. The grown-ups make them sick. The grown-ups go: 'Coo, coo, coo, tickle, tickle, coo,' and they tickle them under the chin. Brinsly laughed aloud.

'What you laughing all by yourself for?' Patricia wanted to know.

'Hi, look! Some boys are having a match,' cried Brinsly suddenly.

'Told you they did,' said Dad from the front seat of the car. 'All by the Greenwich Park, they play.'

'This is still Charlton,' said Patricia, who wanted to show off what she had been learning at school. 'Up to by the Catholic school is Charlton Village. Then we come to Blackheath Standard, then to Greenwich Park, see?'

By Greenwich Park, Brinsly watched longingly. There were dozens of football teams practising. Some were practising in their ordinary clothes. Some had white shorts and colours on. Others were grown men playing with their sons. But some were grown men playing with other grown men.

'Eh, Dad?'

'Yes?'

'Can we stop for a while? Just to watch a little bit, oh please!'

'Why should we?' cried Patricia.

'Your aunty is waiting,' said Mother.

'Maybe a few minutes wouldn't harm us,' said Dad, and pulled into a side street.

'We'll never get there today!' said Patricia, sourly.

'We will. We can get there anytime. It's not a party. We don't have to get there in time,' said Brinsly.

'That's right,' said Dad, and got out.

'I still think that we should go on,' said Mother, but she got out as well.

'And it's going to rain,' said Patricia.

'It isn't!' cried Brinsly.

'There's a cloud,' Patricia pointed.

'The sun looks like it's gone too,' said Mother.

But the family walked across the green and stood watching.

'That's Charlton's colours, Dad,' Brinsly pointed.

'They must be Charlton supporters having a game of their own,' said Dad.

Mother and Patricia had gone to sit on the grass. Patricia was sulking.

'Foul! Foul!' cried Brinsly. 'That man, he fouled, that short man.'

'Who say it's a foul?' cried a big boy and came to stare at Brinsly.

'Eh, it's not a foul,' said Brinsly's dad quickly.

'It is, Dad, I saw it! He tripped the other man on purpose. Look! There he goes again!'

'Who say it's a foul?' Now there were four boys staring at Brinsly.

'Let him talk if he wants to!' cried Patricia from the grass. 'It's his mouth.'

'We *must* go now,' said Mother as she came to stand by Dad and Brinsly.

'Oh, let's go and watch that other game, then we'll go,' said Dad, and he led the way to another side of the green.

'That's right,' said a big boy. 'You better take your family and go, sir.' The boy began to chew and gave Brinsly a nasty look.

'But he did foul,' Brinsly insisted.

'Brinsly, let's go.' Dad hurried and dragged Brinsly away.

Brinsly was still muttering when they got to the other team. 'He *is* a cheater. I wouldn't want to play with cheaters. All the players in Charlton are cheaters. We all know it at school.'

'Now, now. Just because one Charlton player is a cheat that don't mean that all Charlton players are cheats,' laughed Dad.

They could not watch the other game for long because Mother kept looking at the sky, and Patricia kept saying that it was going to rain.

In the end they went off to Aunt Doreen's house. At first they thought that Aunt Doreen had gone out.

'But where?' asked Patricia.

'Let's go! She's out!' said Brinsly, getting ready to leave.

But Patricia rang the doorbell once more. Then Aunt Doreen came to the door.

Aunt Doreen looked terrible, thought Brinsly. She looked very ill.

'Been in the back room. Didn't hear the bell.'

Sadly, Brinsly went in. For a moment he had hoped that his aunt was out and they would all go back home.

As soon as they got in, Brinsly heard the baby screaming at the top of its voice.

'Just as I thought,' said Brinsly under his breath, but his aunt heard him.

'Eh?'

'He says now that he hates babies,' said Patricia.

'Oh?' said Aunt Doreen as she picked up the screaming bundle.

At once Mother and Patricia began to make cooing sounds to the baby.

Brinsly watched and thought that the poor baby must think that grown-ups are silly people. All of them going: 'Coo, coo, lullulu . . .'

Dad and Aunt Doreen began to talk. Mother and Patricia were fussing over the screaming baby, so Brinsly made to slip out.

'Hi, where are you off to?' asked Dad.

'Just to look around. Eh, may I have that ice-cream?'

Dad fished in his pocket and gave Brinsly some change.

'Don't go too far,' said Dad.

'And don't worry bringing ice-cream for the baby,' Aunt Doreen laughed.

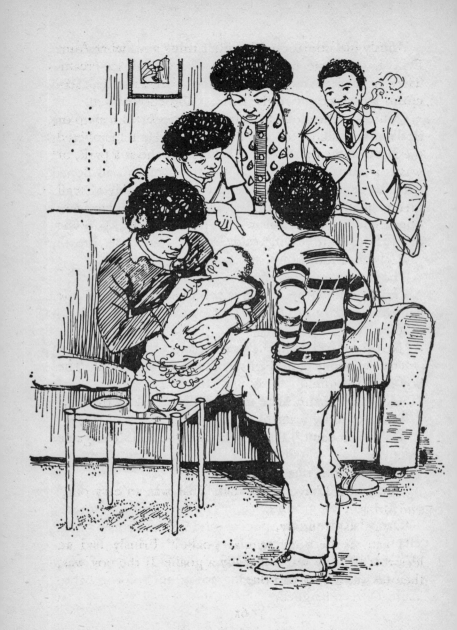

Brinsly did not laugh. He didn't think that what Aunt Doreen said was funny. No baby can eat ice-cream. They open their mouths too wide to scream. The ice-cream would go down their throat and choke them.

Outside in the street Brinsly did not look for a shop or an ice-cream man. He looked for a park. He remembered the last time he came here, they had gone past a park, or was it a green field?

He went up a hill, then he saw it. It was only a small green, smaller than the Greenwich one, but there were boys there playing. Brinsly ran up. He was lucky. Some of the boys were playing football.

'Hi! Can I join in?'

The boys continued to play.

Brinsly walked up to a boy who was waiting for the ball to come to him.

'Can I have a game?'

'No! Push off!' said the boy, rudely.

The ball came near Brinsly. He tried to kick it. The boy grabbed him.

'Hi, you want to taste me knuckles?' asked the boy.

'Oh no. I only want to play.'

'Well, you can't.' The boy kicked the ball. The game went on.

Suddenly someone scored.

'Oh, I could have saved that. That was an easy one,' said Brinsly.

'You?' asked a boy.

'I can. Is he your regular goalie?' Brinsly had an idea that the boy was not really a goalie. If the boy was, then he was a very bad one.

'No. Our goalie couldn't come.'

'I'm a goalie.' Brinsly ran behind the boy, but made sure that he did not try to kick the ball without the boy's permission.

'This kid say he's a goalie,' someone called.

'Well, give him a game,' said one boy.

'No,' said another. 'He doesn't live round here.'

'My aunty does, and my new cousin, and I come here sometimes.' Brinsly badly wanted to have at least one little game. Just one little one.

At first none of the boys wanted Brinsly to join in, but one said, 'I say let him try.'

The other boys still didn't seem to want Brinsly to play but they looked as if they were afraid of the tall boy.

'O.K. Let the kid have a go in goal.'

At once, Brinsly got to work. He worked hard. He tried and dived. The boys were older than he was and had longer legs but he tried hard. Once or twice the boy who was goalie in the first place kicked Brinsly on purpose, but Brinsly went on.

He saved a lot of goals but some balls got in somehow. When he saved a goal the other men in his team cheered. But when a ball went in they called him names. 'Idiot!' they'd shout, or, 'Get him out the goal. He's no good!'

'He is,' said the tallest boy, so Brinsly played on and tried his best.

'He needs more practice, that's all. He's only a kid,' said a grown man who had been watching the game from the grass.

Brinsly played on. He was tired and his shirt was soaking wet, yet he played on. In the end, he noticed that the boys he was playing with had caught up. The score was now seven–seven, so it was a draw.

'We got a good goal scorer, but not a good goalie,' said one boy.

The game stopped. It was getting too dark to play. Not until the game had stopped did Brinsly realize that he had been gone for a long time.

'Oh, I must go back,' he said.

Suddenly he thought, 'Which way did I come?' He looked round. There were many streets all round the green. Was it left or right, or was it straight ahead? And was his dad looking for him at that very moment?

Most of the players had gone. Brinsly noticed the tall boy leaving. He ran and caught up with him. Brinsly was ashamed though to say that he did not know which way he came.

'Eh, I don't live round here, and I ...' he stammered.

'I ain't got no money to give you for bus fare, mate!' said the boy.

'Oh, I've got me own money.'

'Money? Let me see.'

Brinsly was just about to show the boy the fifteen pence when he remembered something Dad had warned him about.

'Why you want to see my money?'

'Just to see how much you got. What you want to buy with it?'

'Eh, nothing. I only want to get back to my aunt. My dad and mum are there, and my sister.'

'Well, go on then. Who's stopping you?'

'I, er, I don't know where it is.'

'Oh, you mean you're lost?'

Brinsly nodded and felt terribly ashamed.

'What's the name of the street?'

'Dallin Road. Oh, not Dallin Road. That is where *I* live.'

'Your aunt's street, dummy! You stupid or something?'

'I, I don't know it.'

'And how you going to get back, stupid, if you don't know the name of the street?'

'There are lots of red houses. I remember that.'

'Oh, Holy Mother. Thousands of red houses round here, boy. If my little buddy was stupid like you, I'd thrash him one.'

'I'm sorry.' Brinsly felt terrible. It was one thing to play good football but another to try and find your aunt's home if you don't even know the name of the street.

'Now, let me think.'

'Maybe we can get to a policeman?'

'Cops? Don't be stupid! They'll throw you in the nick, idiot!'

'But I must get back. My mum, she'll be worried.'

'Let me think. Let's go to the shop and buy some sweets. I think better when I'm sucking a sweet, or chewing gum!'

They got to a corner shop where there was a sweet machine. There was also a chocolate machine but it had been kicked in and all the chocolates were gone.

'Now, give me the money.'

'No, eh, all right.' Brinsly gave him two pence.

The boy soon got some sweets. He got to chewing, too.

'Now, what did you see when you came to your aunt's place? Which bus did you come on?'

'We came in my dad's car.'

'Which way did you come? Where did you come from?'

'From Plumstead, then Shooters Hill. We came by Greenwich Park. You know. Lots of people play football there.'

'Do they?'

'Oh, hundreds.'

'Must get there sometime.'

'Be careful with them Charlton boys though. They cheat and bully.'

'Not me. They wouldn't bully me, can tell you that. Anyway, kid, we better take you to me mum and see what she can do. Watch it. She'll start shouting at me from the door, but she's all right, like.'

The lights were on when they got to the boy's house. His mother was shouting at him because he had stayed out all afternoon, and he hadn't eaten before he went.

'And who is this little boy?'

'He's been goalie for me, now he can't find his aunt's place.'

'Oh, my Lord! What is the name of the street, son?'

'I don't know.' Brinsly felt that if he was not careful he was going to cry.

'Now don't worry, son. Don't you worry. You get him something to eat. Hurry up! Don't stand there!'

'Nothing to eat, please. I only want to get home. I've been away a long time.'

For a moment Brinsly wondered if he was dreaming again. He pinched himself. He was *not* dreaming.

'Look, your aunt got a telephone?'

'Not at her house. She got one at her hospital, but she doesn't go to work now. She's got a new baby. It cries a lot.'

'Oh, your aunt is a nurse, or what?'

Brinsly nodded.

'Now we're getting somewhere. Which hospital? I know all the nurses and orderlies who live round here.'

'Lewisham. That's it. Lewisham General.'

'Oh, that's not local. Oh dear! Is she living in flats, very high flats?'

'I know! I remember. There were very high flats near by, and some of them not finished yet. I remember now. They've got like wheel-barrows on a high stand. Don't know what it is called.'

'Brewer Street! Your aunt lives near Brewer Street. Let's go.'

'Can I come?' the tall boy asked.

'No, you stay with your little brother and sister.'

Soon they were going down some stone steps and walking in a long street where some flats were going up.

'Now, we'll walk up and down the street and we'll ask people. You sure you're not hungry, son?'

'No, I'm not. I just want to get home.'

They walked up the road and saw some girls sitting on a wall. The lady spoke to them.

'A man and his wife been asking if we saw some kid. He ran away. He likes football, the man said.'

'That's me.'

'Where did they go?'

'Don't know,' said one girl.

'By the alley,' said another girl.

'Oh yes, I did go by an alley before I went up a tiny hill.'

'Good!'

The lady then walked up towards the alley. And that's where they found Dad. He was talking to two men and he looked worried.

'Dad! Dad!' called Brinsly.

Dad turned round and saw him. 'You, boy! Where the hell you been, eh? Boy, what I will do to you to-night!'

'Been playing football, and it got late.'

'Now, he was at my house most of the time,' said the lady. 'We had to try and find the street. He didn't know the name.'

'Oh lady! This boy and football. He'll go to Scotland to play football.'

'I know. Same with my boy. He left his food to go to football.'

The lady then said good-bye and left.

Dad took Brinsly to Aunt Doreen's. Mother was really angry.

'I'm sick with you and your football,' said Mother.

'Me too,' said Patricia. 'We could have got home by now, and I want to watch something on telly . . .'

'I got lost,' said Brinsly. 'Anybody can get lost.'

'I never get lost,' shouted Patricia.

'Oh, give him a chance,' said Aunt Doreen.

The family then left for home, with Mother still angry. On the way home Brinsly got a talking-to from Dad. He was told that he should not play football with strangers, and then go to their house.

'And in your good clothes. Now, look at you, you're filthy!' said Mother.

'He should not play any more football if he gets in any more trouble,' said Patricia, spitefully.

'Well, I won't get in any more trouble.'

'Never, ever?' asked Dad.

'No,' Brinsly promised.

'O.K. then. All is forgiven,' laughed Dad.

'He'll get in more trouble all right. You wait and see,' said Patricia.

'I won't!'

'You will!'

'That's enough!' said Mother to Patricia. 'You're no saint!'

The family got back home, and Brinsly tried his best to be good. He even polished the shoes Dad wore to work. Then he went to bed. In bed he planned what he'd tell the men when he saw them at school. He'd give them a good talking-to. After all, Nevil had made him captain of the team. Well, a captain must tell the men off if they don't turn up for practice. So first thing tomorrow . . .

'First thing tomorrow,' thought Brinsly before he closed his eyes, 'I'll tell them off good and proper.'

13 New Colours

The next morning was Monday and the first lesson was art. Brinsly was on duty so he got in early and got all the brushes out. He spread old newspaper on the desks and was filling the cups with water when Mark came.

'Hi, Brins, heard you been playing with the Popapoulos boys, and you saying how you didn't want them in our team. Now you're playing with them behind our backs.'

'I didn't play behind your backs. I went to practise and they were the only men there, that's all.'

'There's Paul now. Hi, Paul, you heard what Brinsly been doing behind our backs?'

'No.'

'Well, he been playing with the Greek brothers.'

'So what?' said Paul.

'They don't live anywhere near Shrewsbury Park,' said Mark.

'Hi, Brin. Hi, Paul,' called Clive.

Just then the bell went for 'in' time. So Brinsly didn't get a chance to say much. He tried to whisper something to Paul during Assembly but Miss Russell, Brinsly's class teacher, was watching him all the time behind those huge spectacles of hers.

After Assembly they had to start painting at once. Paul and Clive were at one end of the room because they were working on a topic. Brinsly was at another end and had no one to work with; this was because Mark was not in Brinsly's group. Mark was in Four B and would be doing extra reading.

Suddenly Brinsly got an idea. He hurried up to Miss Russell. 'May I speak to Paul and Clive for a moment, miss?'

'What's so important? Can't it wait till break? Paul and Clive have to finish the police topic for the competition, you know.'

'Just wanted someone to help me with a new topic.'

'Not another new topic, Brinsly! You're always starting on new topics and then you leave them half-finished to start something else.'

'I wouldn't this time, miss. Honest. It's a football topic, see.'

'We've done hundreds of football topics; no more football topics. I'm sorry. Go on and finish that painting you've been working on.'

'But, miss, I only want to make up a flag like, a banner, for our new team.'

'New team? What new team?'

'We're starting a new team, you ask Paul, miss.'

'That's true,' said Denos.

'You're not in it,' Brinsly barked.

'Oh, I've had enough of new football teams. You go and finish that painting.'

'But, miss.'

'Do as you're told, Brinsly,' said Miss Russell.

Sadly, Brinsly got on with his painting. It was a monster which looked like a dog with three heads. They had been told the story in class and they all had to do some paintings. The others had finished their paintings long ago. But Brinsly just could not finish his. And Miss Russell had said that this time Brinsly must finish this painting before he went on to something else. Brinsly got another of his ideas. If he hurried and finished the painting of this three-headed dog and did it nicely, Miss Russell would then let him do something else. He'd do an emblem for the team. He'd design a scarf. Red and white. No, he thought. Too many teams had red and white. He wanted something new, for a new team.

In the end, Brinsly thought that mauve and white would be best. It would be a little bit unusual and new. The boys could get their mums and sisters, even grandmas to knit scarves in mauve and white. And hats too in mauve and white. They'd then wind the scarves round their necks, and put the hats on their heads. The fans could carry a banner saying: *Shrewsbury killers*. No, the *Shrewsbury Devils*. No, the *Shrewsbury devils ride again* ...

'Brinsly, what on earth!' cried Miss Russell.

'Oh,' Brinsly stared at what Miss Russell was staring at.

'What on earth have you been painting?'

'Oh, I'm sorry, miss, I didn't know I was painting in.'

Suddenly the whole class began to jeer.

'The monster in the book didn't have a scarf round his neck, did it, miss?' asked a girl called Dawn.

'He didn't have a hat on his head, either, I should say,' said Miss Russell staring harshly at Brinsly.

'I'll start over again ... oh, the bell,' said Brinsly sadly.

'You've wasted paper and paint. You're wasteful, Brinsly, and you know it!'

'Start clearing up, everybody,' said Brinsly because he wanted to get out of trouble.

But most of the art things were already cleared away and Brinsly didn't even notice.

'Mh,' Miss Russell was still looking at the mess Brinsly had made of his painting. 'Not like the one in the book, but it does look interesting, I must say.'

'Oh, can I keep it then, miss? I'll take it home and next week I'll start another painting about the story we've heard.'

'Everybody finished that one years ago,' jeered Clive.

'Yes, you may take this one home,' said Miss Russell.

It was then play time. All the children went to play except for Brinsly. He had to put the brushes and things away first.

When he was finished, it was almost 'in' time again,

so Brinsly just had enough time to tell Clive and Paul that they could have a practice that afternoon.

'Good,' said Clive. 'Against the Popapoulos. We'll beat them.'

'No, on our own. Just practising passing and things,' said Brinsly.

'Nah, that's boring. I just want to play the game. I don't want to practise passing and all those things,' said Clive.

'Me too,' said Paul.

It was 'in' time and they had more lessons. Maths, then dinner, then more games in the playground. They had a five-a-side match against the Popapoulos brothers. The brothers won, of course, four goals to nil against Brinsly's team.

But Brinsly did not feel too badly. With practice, he'd win yet.

He took his funny painting home. He did not even get angry when Patricia and her friends jeered and said how stupid the thing looked.

'Three-headed dog with a scarf round its neck, how funny,' they jeered. 'How funny!'

'And with a hat on,' laughed Mother when she saw it. She did not jeer, though, she only said that it looked a bit funny, that's all. In Guyana where she came from and where Brinsly's grandma lived, dogs only had one head. And they never wore hats.

14   The Game
with Charlton

The following Saturday was the first of six weeks of hard work. Often Brinsly had to knock for all the others. Clive often could not come. Sometimes Paul could not come either. The only people who came every one of the six weeks were Brinsly, Denos and the other Popapoulos brothers.

Then on the seventh Saturday they had to play against the Charlton School under tens.

Brinsly was sure that the school cheated because some of those boys were too big to be under ten years old. The boys brought their sisters along to shout and boo. There were dads too. One dad started the trouble that followed. He kept shouting that the referee was biased.

'Ref, you blind or something? Foul, foul!' shouted the dad and began to shake his fist. 'Get that boy off, or I'll come and get him off myself.'

It was not a foul though and the referee, who was a teacher from the Shrewsbury Park Comprehensive, let the game go on.

Then came an accident. Denos accidentally tripped the centre forward of Charlton. The forward got angry and punched Denos. But Denos' brothers didn't like to see their brother get punched. So one of them punched back.

Everybody started punching then. The referee blew his whistle. He stopped the punching but the dad who had been shouting 'foul' had by then got on the field.

'That boy started it,' said the dad and pushed Denos.

Denos' uncle saw him and ran out on the field. He shouted, 'Hi, why you going pushing little kids for?'

'Inside!' shouted the referee to all the men.

'Quick,' shouted one of the linesmen who was a big boy from the school up the hill.

Brinsly and all his men hurried to the hut by the Shrewsbury Library. This hut was loaned to them for use as a dressing-room.

Nevil came in then and said, 'Disgusting. Grown men behaving like that? Grown men.'

'On T.V. it's the kids who start punch-ups,' laughed Denos. He was not angry at all.

'Yeh,' said Brinsly. 'But here it's a dad who started it and all because Charlton was losing.'

'Yeh,' said Denos, 'we were going to thrash them, good and proper.'

'Yeh,' said Paul, 'I reckon that we could have scored ten goals, if we wanted to.'

'Them no good,' laughed Errol. 'You beat them any time.' Errol could not play under tens.

Soon the trainer from the other team came to the dressing-room. He apologized. 'They didn't mean no harm, just a bit of fun,' he laughed.

'Fun? You're bad losers,' said Nevil.

'Yes, you are,' said Brinsly.

'We can play again,' said the trainer of Charlton.

'Any time,' said Denos in a nasty manner.

77

'Not if your boys play like that. They were fouling all the time,' said Nevil.

'Well,' laughed the trainer, 'let's say they tackle, well, a bit too hard. I'll speak to them about that.'

'You do that,' said Nevil.

'We'll play at our ground; of course, it depends on our manager . . .'

'No,' shouted Denos. 'You'll beat us up when you lose.'

'Now, let me handle this, Denos,' said Nevil.

'Oh, tell you what, we don't mind playing you here. Well, since we'll be in the final for the Greenwich Festival under ten trophy, we may well have to play you here. That is, if you don't get knocked out in the early rounds . . .' The trainer then pulled a nasty face and turned away.

'I hate him,' said Denos, as soon as the trainer had gone. 'My uncle can smash his teeth in, any time.'

'What's this about the Greenwich Festival?' asked Brinsly.

'Oh, it's in June.'

'June is a long time away, eh, we got March to go . . .' began Paul.

'Then April, then May . . .' said Clive.

'Then June,' said Mark.

They began to walk back home.

'Are we going to enter?' asked Brinsly.

'Depends, we . . . we don't always turn up for practice,' said Nevil.

'We will, won't we?' said Paul.

'You better,' said Denos.

Denos stared at Brinsly and Brinsly nodded. 'Yes, I'll knock at his place and get him out.'

'You do that,' said Denos. 'And I'll get Mark and the rest out. And maybe my cousin can bring us all in his car.'

The others went off and Brinsly and Denos were left talking. Suddenly, Brinsly felt that there was something he had to say to Denos.

'Eh, sorry I didn't want you to join this team.'

'Oh, didn't you?' shrugged Denos and went off to join his brothers going down the hill towards their home.

Watching him go Brinsly thought, 'He can play, together we will make a good team if only he didn't have to brag so much. And things . . .'

Still thinking, Brinsly got home to find that there were some errands he had to do. 'Oh why can't Patricia do it, Mum?'

'No!' shouted Patricia. 'I've got to knit your scarves, remember?'

'Oh that.' Suddenly Brinsly didn't mind running errands if it meant that Patricia would be knitting his scarves – one for him and one for Clive. Clive had no one to knit it for him. His mother could not knit and his sister didn't knit either.

'O.K., O.K., I'll go.' So, though tired and hungry, Brinsly went off.

He ran most of the time and when he returned home he found Nevil there talking to his father.

'Oh, hi, Brin. Had to come and get your particulars.'
'What?'

'Name, age and so on. I found out that we've got to register now if we want to enter the festival.'

'Are we going to enter, then? Are we?'

'Not sure yet, but we better register to say that we will. And if, by the time of the festival, we're not up to form, we can always back out.'

'But if you don't sign in at all and you find that you're up to form you will not be able to enter,' said Brinsly's father.

'We will, you wait and see, we will,' said Brinsly, forgetting that he was so hungry and thirsty.

Nevil was not too sure. 'It will mean hard work. Work-outs and practices, and then the scarves to be knitted. And we need a proper name for our team. At present I'll put down *Shrewsbury Boys*. And we better put down ten and under because of Denos. He may be ten before the festival and we don't want to lose Denos, nor cheat about his age.'

'No, we must not cheat. We must win fair and square.'

'Oh, another thing, we need to know soon about the colours,' said Nevil.

'I thought, eh, what about mauve and white. That's the colours my sister is knitting for me and Clive. Sorry, didn't get a chance to tell you.'

'That's great. Mauve and white, eh, and your sister is knitting.'

'She is, been knitting till late at night,' said Dad with a smile.

'Pat! Patricia! Bring your knitting for Nevil to see,' called Brinsly.

'Coming.'

Soon Patricia was showing off her knitting.

'Good. Fantastic. My little sister can't knit like that,' said Nevil.

'Good, Patricia can teach her, can't you, Pat?' said Brinsly.

'But ...'

'Of course you can,' said Dad.

'She can come here,' said Brinsly, 'and you two can knit all the scarves and hats.'

'Oh dear,' said Mother from the doorway.

'And the mums can make cakes for tea after, can't you, Mum?'

'You're trying to get everybody in, aren't you?' laughed Mother.

'Oh, and we'll need some sort of emblem, won't we? I, oh, wait!' Brinsly ran upstairs, got his painting off the wall.

He ran back downstairs, taking two steps at a time.

'Hi, you'll break your leg and you won't be able to play at all,' warned Dad.

'Who, who did this?' asked Nevil.

'I did. But it's not very good.'

'The idea is good. But we must find a reason for having a three-headed monster. Maybe your teacher can find a reason.'

'Maybe, all the school kids can have a competition and say why the team has a three-headed monster!' said Dad.

'You like it then?' Brinsly asked Nevil.

'Mhh,' said Nevil.

'I think it looks stupid,' said Patricia.

'Be quiet,' said Mother.

'But if I'm going to knit things for them, I don't want the girls to laugh at me. They'll say that my brother's team has some stupid three-headed monster.'

'Not if the monster means something,' said Nevil.

'See, see?' said Brinsly.

'I must go now,' said Nevil. 'But remember, hard work from now on and we better meet on Tuesday afternoon as well. Can you come on Tuesday? The others said that they can.'

'Oh, yes, and Sunday morning. I used to play with the Popapoulos brothers and their dads and uncles. You can come too, Dad.'

'Oh, dear, he won't be satisfied until the whole family is in,' laughed Mother and said good-bye to Nevil.

After Nevil had gone, Brinsly did a few head-stands and cartwheels.

'It'll be great!' he said. 'We'll win the Greenwich trophy, for sure. We'll thrash them Charlton boys, that'll teach them. Think the newspaper people would come?'

'Which newspaper? Newspapers don't care about your stupid team,' said Patricia.

'Of course they do.' Brinsly jumped on a chair. 'Everybody'll cheer: "Come on, goalie, *clap clap*. Come on, goalie, *clap clap* . . .""'

'Get down before you fall over!'

'I'll be famous. Perhaps someone would kidnap you, Dad, and say I must not play in such or such a match or they'll shoot you.'

'Brinsly, stop that, want to break your neck?' shouted Mother.

'I won't, Mum. Got to keep my neck, at least until after the festival,' said Brinsly.

Still feeling very happy, he thought, 'I'll practise so hard that we'll get through all the qualifying games . . . and . . .'

15   The Trophy

Brinsly did work very hard. He had many problems. There were the times when there were only himself and the Popapoulos brothers. Then when there was some freak cold weather, he was so cold that he could not stop or hold the ball, and his team had lost two matches. After losing the second match, even Brinsly's best friends stopped speaking to him. They blamed him for the goals scored against the team.

Soon the weather got better though and the Shrewsbury boys began to win. They won all the qualifying matches and got through to the final. The trouble was that they were playing against Charlton, who now called themselves the *White Panthers*. They, the *White Panthers*, had often won their matches by really thrashing the other team. Once they got as much as eleven goals to nil.

As the final day got nearer, Brinsly got really scared. Once he even wished that he'd get the measles so he wouldn't have to play.

'They'll blame me if we lose,' he told his dad, his sister and his mother.

But Brinsly didn't get the measles and the day of the big match was there. All the hats were ready because parents at the school got together and helped. Every fan had a mauve and white hat and scarf. Even baby brothers and dads were busy. And the mums were getting tea after the game.

Brinsly went to see the Shrewsbury Park pitch and thought that it looked great. Mother thought that it looked as if a carnival was about to take place – flags, balloons, banners and posters, too.

There was even a grandstand where all the old ladies and old gentlemen round Shrewsbury Park would sit and watch the Shrewsbury boys win.

Then came the morning of the game. The kick-off was at eleven sharp. But the men and other helpers were to get there earlier.

Dad had to take Mother to the Woolwich market to get some last-minute things, he said. So Brinsly had to get dressed and go by himself. Dad and Mother would follow. Patricia too had to leave early because she and her friend were cheer leaders. They were to dress up in short mauve skirts and white blouses. They were meeting at Shrewsbury House. The Plumcraft Boy Scouts were going to play and the Brownies were to be majorettes. The lady mayoress would come to present the trophy.

'Hurry, hurry!' Brinsly told himself that morning. He was already dressed by ten o'clock. He thought that he had better be going by ten-thirty though it was only a ten minute walk to the pitch. He shined his boots for what could have been the hundredth time. He checked his kit, as he had done at least a dozen times. Then, at a few minutes before ten-thirty, he decided to walk slowly to the pitch.

'I'm not scared of them,' he told himself again and again. Then he slammed the front door behind him.

He soon reached the corner by the new flats. He saw a car coming. He was going to walk on, but the car stopped alongside him.

There were three young men, about seventeen years old, in the car. One leaned back and asked, 'Where is number sixty Dallin Road?'

'Up there, but there's no one in.'

'How do you know?' said one young man, he could have been a big boy instead of a young man.

'That's where I live.'

'Is your brother a, eh, Brinsly, and a goalie for them, eh, Shrewsbury lot?'

'It's not my brother, it's me.'

'Good, jump in!' laughed the first young man.

'What for?' Brinsly suddenly remembered his dad warning him never to go in strangers' cars.

'I'm Nevil's cousin and he sent me to fetch you,' said the second young man. He, too, looked more like a big boy than a young man.

'Are you? And why ...' Brinsly did not hesitate further, he got in the car before he finished that sentence. In the car he continued. 'Why has he sent to fetch me?'

'He wants you all to get there earlier.'

'Hi ... Hi, you're going the wrong way!' Brinsly cried suddenly.

'That's a better way, see,' said the big boy.

Suddenly this big boy no longer looked friendly. He began to chew, although he had no chewing-gum in his mouth.

'He's trying to scare me, but I'm not scared,' thought Brinsly.

'Stop, and let me out!'

Brinsly tried to reach the little black knob on the door handle. He knew that it was a safety lock and he would not be able to open the door without pressing it down. Brinsly never got that knob down. The big boy on his left grabbed him hard, and pressed him down on the seat.

'You're hurting me,' shouted Brinsly.

'Hi, man, no rough stuff, hear? Not hurting no little

kids,' said the driver of the car. He had not spoken until then. And he looked a little bit older than the other two.

'Where you taking me? You must have got the wrong boy. I haven't done anything. My dad has no money, honest,' said Brinsly.

'Shut up!' said the big boy on his right.

'Hi, you're going too fast, you'll kill somebody,' said Brinsly.

'Keep your head down, or I'll slice your throat, get it?' said one big boy.

'But what d'you want with me?'

Brinsly knew that they were now at traffic lights. He tried to raise his head but the big boy on the left twisted his wrist very hard and pinned him down.

'Keep your head down,' said the first big boy.

'And shut your cake hole, will you,' said the other.

'No rough stuff, or I quit,' said the driver.

'Well, tell him to shut up,' said one big boy.

'Shut up, brother. No one will hurt you. Just having a bit of fun. O.K.?'

'Fun? I got to . . . Oh no, I'll be late!' cried Brinsly.

'Clever boy . . . who's a clever boy then?' mocked one big boy.

'You want me to be late on purpose.'

'Yep, just a tiny bit late though. You'll get there just in time to see the Charlton boys take the trophy.'

'Oh, you're . . . you . . . you're cheating.'

'Shut up. I get nervous when snotty little kids start whining. I get very nervous,' said one big boy.

Suddenly, Brinsly got an idea. He was dreaming! 'That's it. Like that time when I dreamt that I got to the pitch in my pyjamas and that Mum was banging a drum. That's it, a dream!'

'Hi, wipe that grin off your face. You try anything and you'll get us all killed.'

Brinsly leaned back his head and just smiled. 'Why worry,' he thought. 'The dream will soon end.'

He would then find that he had not got up at all yet. But he did get up. Surely he couldn't dream about Mother going off to the market and Patricia going to get dressed for cheer leading.

But the dream went on for a long time. Brinsly felt as if they were driving round and round. He was sure that they had gone past that particular monument at least three times. Or there could be three different monuments.

He thought of the big boys beside him falling asleep. Then he'd jump out. Even in dreams you can jump out. But the big boys did not sleep. One kept looking at his watch. Then, when he thought it was time to go home, he said to his friend, 'Right, this is it.'

'What's your name?' asked Brinsly for no particular reason.

'What I want to go tell you me name for? Think I'm stupid or something?'

'He's Nevil's cousin, tell Nevil that,' laughed the other big boy.

'Yeh, his friendly cousin, who lives in Charlton village, get that? And he told me to come and get you?'

'You're lying. Why should he want me to get – be late? It's gone eleven.'

Suddenly, Brinsly began to wonder if this really was a dream. Maybe it was, maybe it wasn't.

'Ask him. Anyhow, we'll drop you here.'

'Aren't you afraid I'll tell the police? They'll come and get you.'

'Tell them what? That Nevil asked his cousin from Charlton to drive you round a tiny bit?' mocked one big boy.

'Nevil wouldn't do that. He trained us, he'll want us to win, see.'

'What if the other team paid him to keep you out?'

'What for? I'm not the only one in the team.'

'Out you go, sonny boy!'

With a sharp bump Brinsly was on the grass and the car drove off turning the corner at great speed. The number! Brinsly thought. He should have taken the number. But it was nearly too late. He just saw *280M* before the car had gone. Brinsly had no idea where he was. He saw a bus go past but it was not one of those he knew by number.

Suddenly, he saw a police panda car. He rushed up without thinking, began to wave frantically. The car stopped with a loud screeching of brakes.

A young policeman jumped out and for a moment Brinsly thought that he looked very much like Nevil. He was not as friendly as Nevil though, for he shouted at Brinsly.

'What the hell you think you're doing? Trying to get yourself killed?'

'Eh, no, I was kidnapped,' said Brinsly.

'Oh god, not another one!' said the second policeman who had now come out of the car. 'These little kids would do anything to try and get a ride in the panda. Suppose you'll want an ice-cream, and sardine sandwiches at the station?'

'Is the truth, please believe me. Got a football match, it should be at eleven.'

'Football match? Eleven? You mean eleven to-night?' said the first policeman.

'Look, son, run along home, will you,' said the second.

'It's true! Two big boys grabbed me; one looked like you, sir.'

'Could be his brother?' mocked the second policeman.

'No, he said he was Nevil's cousin, or his friend, I can't remember. But you must take me quick, please. The others are not very good in goal, you see, please, sir.'

'Eh, you said you were on your way to a football match?'

'Yes, I'm the goalie, see.'

'Where are your football things – your kit, I mean?' asked the first policeman.

'Oh, no! It's still in the car! They chucked me out, and I forgot the kit.'

'Funny footballer, forgetting his kit,' said the second policeman.

The policemen then moved to get back in the car.

'Please!' cried Brinsly. 'Take me to the Shrewsbury Park pitch and see for yourself. It's up by Shooters Hill, see!'

'Boy, do you know how much money your parents will have to pay if you waste policemen's time?' asked the first policeman.

'I don't know, but please hurry.'

The second policeman shrugged, then they let Brinsly in.

'I'll sit behind with him,' said the first policeman.

Without anything further said, they drove off. Brinsly

was surprised to see how quickly they got to the top of Shooters Hill. He then realized that he had not been far away from Shooters Hill at all; the only thing was that he didn't know that area.

'There it is, see, all the banners, see,' said Brinsly.

Brinsly tried to open the door and rush out but the first policeman stopped him. He drove right up to where the mayoress was just about to present the prize.

'Who won?' Brinsly asked as soon as they got out.

'Shrewsbury got thrashed. Their goalie never turned up, he chickened out,' said a grown-up boy. The boy had taken off his mauve and white scarf but had forgotten to take off his hat.

'But that's cheating, eh, I mean,' Brinsly stammered.

People were cheering the Charlton boys.

Brinsly forgot all about the policemen and ran up to the stand. 'I was kidnapped!' he shouted.

'That's Brinsly,' shouted someone and then a whole crowd shouted.

'That's that goalie. He turned up at the end.'

'You've got to believe me,' Brinsly begged.

There came a murmur in the crowd by the stand. An old lady got up. She was shaking a little but someone helped her to stand up. She whispered something to the old man sitting next to her.

There was a lot of whispering among the people. Then they spoke to the policemen.

The policemen spoke to the lady who was going to present the trophy.

Suddenly the man sitting next to the mayoress spoke through the loudspeaker:

'Ladies and gentlemen, your attention, please. There seems to be a mistake. The goalie of Shrewsbury boys had been seen being taken in a car. This lady here, Mrs Taylor, saw it.'

'Oh, they planned it. We won!' shouted someone.

Again the grown-ups whispered. Nevil came and spoke too. During that time Brinsly went to talk to the other men of his team. They at first didn't believe him. But later they did. Brinsly would never plan to run off. And Nevil had been working very hard, he wouldn't want the team to lose. So, of course, he did not send anyone to kidnap Brinsly.

Suddenly, a voice came over the loudspeaker again. This time it was the manager of the other side speaking, 'Ladies and gentlemen, may I say how deeply sorry I am that this has happened. But someone, someone who badly wanted Charlton to win, has played what they may have considered a little joke on the Shrewsbury boys. I can promise you that we'll find out who is behind it . . .'

'Replay!' shouted one of the Shrewsbury fans.

'Replay. The match has got to be replayed,' the whole crowd chanted.

'Replay, a replay!'

Someone began to wave a mauve and white hat.

'Replay for the trophy festival trophy.'

'Replay!'

The manager tried to speak again but the noise was too much. Everyone was shouting. Balloons went up. The Boy Scouts began to play again. Fans rushed out to speak to Brinsly. Girls were pushing, grown-ups were